To anyone who's ever taken a selfie: your stories matter.
Keep being yourself, unfiltered. —S. G. M.

To friends, who make life a lot more fun. —F. W.

STERLING CHILDREN'S BOOKS
New York

An Imprint of Sterling Publishing Co., Inc.
1166 Avenue of the Americas
New York, NY 10036

ISBN 978-1-4549-2129-5

Distributed in Canada by Sterling Publishing Co., Inc.
c/o Canadian Manda Group, 664 Annette Street
Toronto, Ontario M6S 2C8, Canada
Distributed in the United Kingdom by GMC Distribution Services
Castle Place, 166 High Street, Lewes, East Sussex BN7 1XU, England
Distributed in Australia by NewSouth Books
45 Beach Street, Coogee, NSW 2034, Australia

For information about custom editions, special sales, and premium and corporate purchases,
please contact Sterling Special Sales at 800-805-5489 or specialsales@sterlingpublishing.com.

Manufactured in China

Lot #:
2 4 6 8 10 9 7 5 3 1
12/17

sterlingpublishing.com

Cover and interior design by Irene Vandervoort

SELFIE
Sebastian

BY **Sarah Glenn Marsh**

ILLUSTRATED BY
Florence Weiser

STERLING CHILDREN'S BOOKS
New York

Sebastian knows he's a good-looking fox.

Really, really good-looking.

*Don't
you
think?*

Sebastian **loves** to take selfies on his adventures in the forest. Here he is

swimming in his favorite **pond** . . .

scaring some **chickens** . . .

and stealing a **pie** from Old Man Pennywhistle's cottage.

He will always remember how tasty it was.

Still, something's wrong with every one of his pictures, and he can't quite put his paw on what's missing. None of his pictures make him as happy as a perfect selfie should.

So, to figure out what's missing, Sebastian has decided that today he will go on a quest to take the perfect selfie.

First, he'll need the **right outfit**.

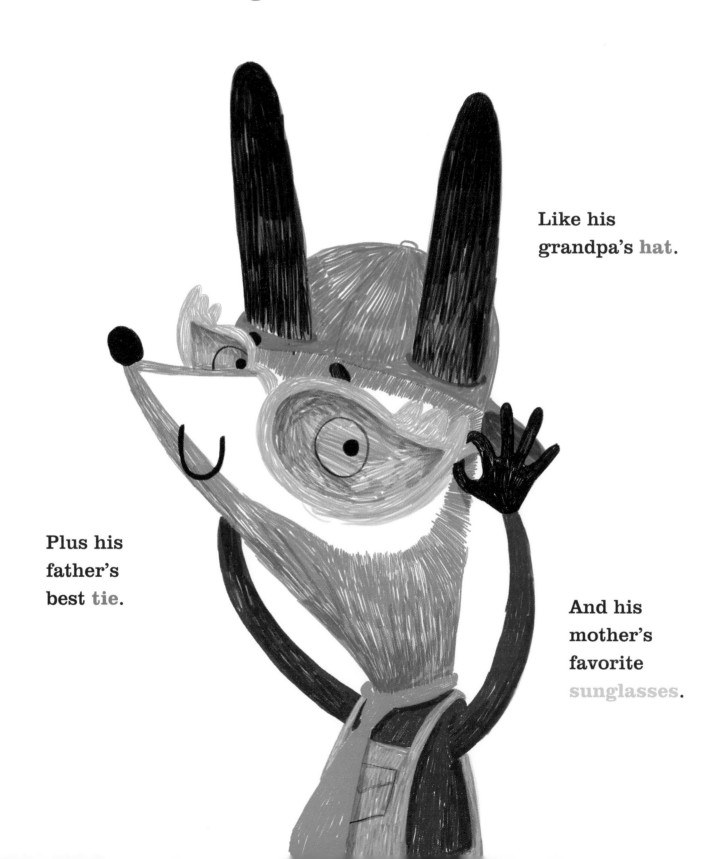

Like his
grandpa's **hat**.

Plus his
father's
best **tie**.

And his
mother's
favorite
sunglasses.

Now he's ready for the camera! But something still doesn't feel right.

As Sebastian gazes around at the walls of his den, he has an idea!

Because none of his selfies in the forest have been
perfect, he decides he needs to go somewhere different.

Sebastian packs a bag, calls good-bye to his friends,
and sets off on his biggest adventure yet.

Sebastian has been **dreaming** of visiting Fun World to take a selfie on the newest roller coaster.

He just didn't realize how hard it would be to hold on to the camera!

Something is still **missing** from his latest selfie, though. A perfect picture would make him happy, and this one just . . . doesn't.

Luckily, Sebastian has a long list of places he has always wanted to see!

He dashes to **Hollywood**, where his movie director uncle gives him free tickets to a big awards show.

The **red carpet** is full of people taking selfies, just like Sebastian!

But even this picture is not perfect. It doesn't make him smile at all.

Sebastian decides he needs to think bigger—*grander*, even.

But this selfie doesn't make him happy either.

Maybe he needs to think . . . *higher*.

Sebastian had forgotten
how scared he is of heights,
but he will do **anything** for
a perfect selfie.

Yet this picture still doesn't make him happy.

He decides to travel even higher, to a place where no fox has dared to go before.

Sebastian always thought the **moon** was made of cheese. But it's not.

It's not so great for taking selfies, either.

It seems no matter where he goes . . .

or what amazing things he does . . .

or how much **fun** everyone else is having around him . . .

. . . Sebastian's selfies are **never** perfect.
None of them make him happy.

He has the right outfit. He's been to the most amazing places and done the most exciting things. And still, *still*, something is missing from all of his pictures.

In fact, he thinks the selfies he took at home were better somehow. So he packs his bag and heads back to the forest.

Home at last, Sebastian raises his camera for one last selfie. He tries his best to put on a happy face. And he snaps a picture.

Sebastian whirls around to see his best
friend, Fred, laughing and smiling.

Sebastian doesn't think there's anything
funny about Fred wrecking his selfie.

But when he looks at the selfie again, it makes him smile
a little. He decides it's actually a pretty good picture.

Fred thinks so, too.

Something about this selfie makes Sebastian **happier** than all the ones he took on his adventures.

And the next one makes him smile even more.

Sebastian tries to put his paw on what's different this time. He's wearing the same outfit. He's in the same old forest where he's taken hundreds of pictures before. Not an exciting place like the moon.

But Fred wasn't there. His *friends* weren't there.

Finally, Sebastian realizes what was missing from his pictures. All around him, he has the secret to taking a selfie that's absolutely . . .

. . . perfect.